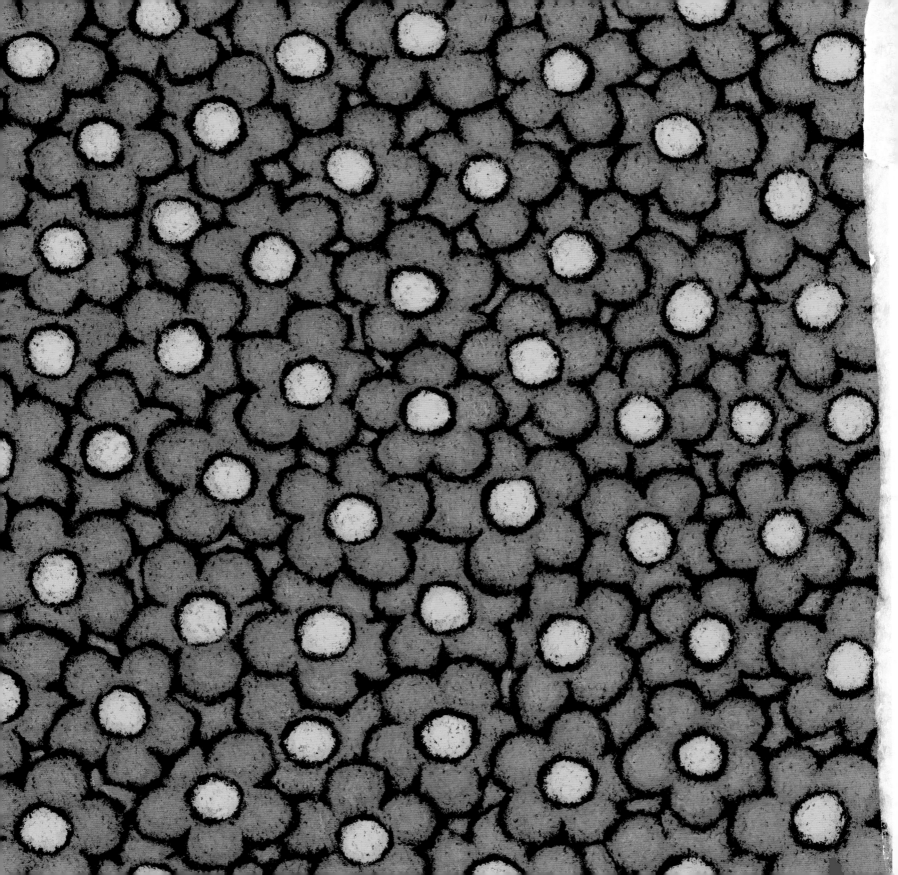

lila prap

Once Upon...

1001

STORIES

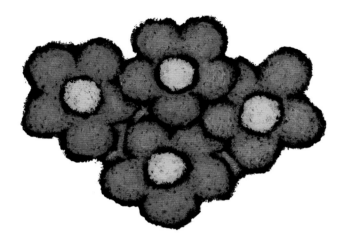

My dear young readers:

If you read this book like you read other books, from the first page right through to the last page, you'll be very confused and think, "What a strange book!" This book is not like other books – this is a different sort of book. At the bottom of each page there are two questions, which let you decide how you'd like the story to continue. Everything depends on your choices.

If you are very curious, and if you like lots of different kinds of adventures, you will find many, many, many stories inside… (maybe even 1001).

I wish you a wonderful journey,

Lila Prap

First American Edition 2006
by Kane/Miller Book Publishers, Inc.
La Jolla, California

Copyright @ Mladinska Knjiga Založba, 2005

First published in Slovenia in 2005 by
Mladinska Knjiga
Slovenska cesta 29, 1000 Ljubljana Slovenia

Library of Congress Control Number: 2005930587
Printed and Bound in China by Regent Publishing Services Ltd.
1 2 3 4 5 6 7 8 9 10
ISBN-13: 978-1-929132-92-8
ISBN-10: 1-929132-92-1

# Lila Prap

## Once Upon...
## 1001
## STORIES

## Kane/Miller
### BOOK PUBLISHERS

Once there was a little girl who was so gentle and so kind that everyone liked her.

Even though the little girl was young, she was a big help to her mother. She liked doing chores around the house, and everything her mother asked her to do she did quickly and with great care.

One day, her mother asked her to take some things to her grandmother, who was sick. Her grandmother lived in a tiny house in the middle of the forest.

"Be very careful!" her mother warned. "Since this is the first time you're going to your grandmother's house by yourself, you must remember to stay on the path. And make sure you do not talk to strangers."

# 1

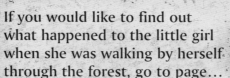 If you would like to find out what happened to the little girl when she was walking by herself through the forest, go to page… **4**

Or, would you be more interested in reading a story about a rude little boy who teased his brothers? If so, go to page… **2**

Once there was a little boy who was so rude and so naughty that nobody liked him. His parents often went out, so the boy's older brothers had to take care of him. The little boy teased his older brothers and made them mad, until one day they'd had enough. They took the fishing pole the little boy had been poking them with and threw it out the door. They threw the little boy out too, and said angrily, "Don't come back until you've caught every single fish in the lake!"

The little boy stood pouting in front of the house for awhile, and then marched off into the forest. There might be somebody in there he could tease!

Are you interested in what happened to the little boy when he went into the forest? Go to page… **13**

Would you be more interested in a different story? Would you like one about three little pigs? Go to page… **19**

**2**

t he three bears had been taking a walk in the forest. They were glad to be back home, but something wasn't right. They sniffed suspiciously, and stood in the middle of their house, their fur on end.

"Somebody's been eating my porridge!" growled the biggest bear in the deepest voice.

"Somebody's been sitting in my chair!" complained the medium-sized bear, in a medium-sized voice.

"Somebody's been sleeping in my bed!" said the littlest bear in the squeakiest voice. "And she's still there!"

The little girl woke up just as the bears were standing over her. She jumped out the window and ran off into the dark forest.

Would you like to know where the little girl went when she ran away from the three bears? Go to page… 21

Or, would you like it better if the little girl was woken up by someone other than the bears? In that case, go to page… 20

t he little girl was skipping merrily along the path through the forest when a big, bad wolf suddenly appeared from behind a tree.

"Where are you going, little girl?" he asked in a sly, sweet voice.

"To my grandmother's house," the little girl told him, and very kindly explained where her grandmother lived and how she was going to get there. She had never seen a big, bad wolf before and so she didn't know to be afraid of him.

"Why don't you pick a nice bunch of flowers for your grandmother, too?" suggested the big, bad wolf. "I think she'd like that."

Would you like to find out what happened when the little girl did what the big, bad wolf suggested? Continue to page… **7**

Would you like it better if the little girl ran away, instead of talking to the big, bad wolf? Then go to page… **6**

4

"I'll catch a million fish and throw them all at my stupid brothers!" muttered the little boy as he walked towards the lake in the middle of the forest. For a long time he didn't catch anything, and he was just about ready to give up when he *finally* managed to catch a teeny, tiny fish.

"If you let me go, I'll grant you three wishes!" promised the teeny, tiny fish.

"I know what I want!" said the little boy, "I want you to turn into an ugly frog!" He threw the teeny, tiny fish back into the water, and marched off into the forest, his fishing pole over his shoulder. (He didn't believe the teeny, tiny fish.) Meanwhile, the teeny, tiny fish was growing. Its eyes were beginning to bulge, and it turned a very peculiar shade of green. Then it hopped away.

5

If you would like to find out what else happened to the little boy in the forest, go to page… **12**

Would you rather learn what happened to the teeny, tiny fish after he was turned into a frog? Go to page… **21**

he little girl ran off into the forest and only stopped when she came to the door of a magnificent castle. The door slowly opened, and the little girl went in, curious to see inside. The castle was beautiful, but there was no one there. She ate a few pieces of food from a very full table in one of the rooms, and fell asleep in a beautiful bed. Over the next few days, everything she wished for appeared. It was very nice, though she soon grew homesick. But, when she tried to leave the castle, a horrible creature blocked her way.

"You must stay here!" he growled. He took the little girl up to the highest room in the castle tower and locked her inside.

Would you like to know if the little girl remained the horrible creature's prisoner forever? Go to page… 16

What would happen if the little girl got away from the horrible creature before he could stop her? Go to page… 11

t he little girl thought it was a very good idea. She started to pick flowers, and as she did so the big, bad wolf ran quickly to the grandmother's house.

He knocked on the door and called in a high voice, "Grandmother, I've brought you a basket of goodies from Mother."

"Come in!" called the grandmother. "The key is between the two flowerpots on the windowsill."

When the door was unlocked and opened, she shrieked in fright. It was a big, bad wolf, not her granddaughter! With one giant leap, he was at her side.

7

Would you like to know why the big, bad wolf went to the grandmother's house? Continue to page…  8

Would you like it better if the big, bad wolf was feeling sick and never reached the grandmother's house? Turn to page…  22

t he big, bad wolf ate the grandmother. Then he put her bonnet on his head and her glasses on his nose, and got into her bed to wait for the little girl.

After awhile, when she had picked so many flowers she almost couldn't carry them, the little girl skipped her way to her grandmother's house. But when she went in, she couldn't help wondering why her grandmother's eyes and ears were so big.

"All the better to see and hear you with, sweetie!"

And what about her mouth?

"All the better to eat you with!" growled the big, bad wolf, and he ate the little girl, too.

Full and happy, he fell asleep in the grandmother's bed, and began to snore.

Did anyone come to rescue the grandmother and the little girl? Find out on page… **12**

Are you unhappy about the big, bad wolf eating the grandmother and the little girl? Should he have found something else to eat? Turn to page… **23**

t he little girl just could not kiss the ugly frog. Instead, she ran off as fast as her legs could carry her and hid inside an empty house in the forest. The frog hopped angrily after her.

"I want a kiss, not a broken promise!" he croaked, standing in front of the door to the house.

The frog would not stop croaking – even to sleep – and after three days and nights, the little girl was very tired and very angry.

"Fine! I'll do what I promised. But then you have to disappear. I never want to see you again!"

She bent down, and with her eyes closed, kissed the frog.

9

Did the little girl get sick after kissing the frog? Did something bad happen? Go to page…  **28**

Would you like it better if the little girl ran into the forest instead of kissing the ugly frog? Go to page…  **6**

the little girl and the little boy left the castle and set off through the forest for home. They walked for a long time and were very tired. Finally, they came across a colorful little house in the middle of a meadow.

"It's made out of cake!" they shouted as they got closer.

They began to tear off and eat pieces of the delicious house, when suddenly, the door opened, and a little old lady appeared on the doorstep.

"Come in!" she said, and invited them to follow her into the house.

"There are even better things to eat inside!"

Would you like to know what the little boy and the little girl found inside? Go to page… **15**

Would you like it better if there was no one living in the house? Then go to page… **27**

At the sight of the horrible creature, the little girl ran screaming past its claws and into the forest. The horrible creature ran after her, but with every step he became smaller and smaller, until suddenly, he turned into a tiny mouse. The tiny mouse became frightened and hid in a small bottle he found lying among the leaves. The little girl saw the bottle top, quickly put it on, and ran deeper into forest.

Then, she stopped when she came to an old house, and quietly stepped inside. There was no one there, but there was some porridge in a dish on the table. She ate it, and then fell asleep in the nearest bed.

**11**

Are you glad that the little girl found the house? Would you like to know who lived there? Go to page… **3**

Or, would you like to find out if the tiny mouse who was stuck in the bottle ever managed to escape? Go to page… **13**

the little boy was wandering aimlessly through the forest when he came upon the grandmother's house. He went in and found the big, bad wolf snoring happily in the grandmother's bed. He could hear shouts for help coming from the wolf's stomach, so he quickly found a pair of scissors and cut the wolf open. Out jumped the grandmother and the little girl. They were very happy to be rescued, and hugged the astonished little boy.

"You should put stones in the big, bad wolf's stomach!" suggested the little boy, as the big, bad wolf began to mumble in his sleep. "That way, he won't be able to eat anyone ever again!" The grandmother and the little girl gathered as many stones as they could find, as the little boy went off into the forest, whistling happily.

Would you like to know what happened when the big, bad wolf woke up full of stones? Go to page… **22**

Would you rather find out what other adventures the little boy had in the forest? Go to page… **16**

**12**

t he little boy, who had managed to knock some birds' nests out of the trees, frighten all the squirrels and rabbits with his shouting, and kick all the mushrooms he found in his way, stopped in front of a large anthill.

He was just about to start poking it with a stick, when his eyes fell on a small bottle, hidden among the leaves. "What's this?" he asked, as he pulled the top off the bottle.

A horrible creature began to climb out. It grew and grew until it was as tall as the tallest tree.

"I'm going to eat you now!" howled the horrible creature as it reached for the little boy.

**13**

What happened to the little boy? Did the horrible creature really eat him? Find out on page… **18**

Would it be better if the boy went fishing instead of doing naughty things in the forest? Go to page… **5**

he little girl stayed with the dwarves for many years, until finally, she was grown up, and very beautiful. One day, while she was busy sweeping, there was a knock at the window. A poor old woman was standing at the front of the house, and even though the dwarves had told her never to speak to strangers, the girl opened the door.

"A very good day to you, my lovely!" cried the old woman. "I'm selling apples." She offered the girl the nicest apple in the basket. The girl was enchanted, and bit into it at once. She immediately fell down as if she were dead. The old woman, who was, in fact, a witch, and who hated all kind and gentle girls, disappeared into the forest, laughing nastily.

**14**

What did the dwarves do when they found the girl? Were they able to help her? Go to page… **26**

Would you like it better if the girl didn't open the door, and the old woman went off into the forest? Go to page… **17**

he old woman was really a witch, and she grabbed the little boy by his collar and locked him in a cage. She took the frightened little girl to the kitchen where she was forced to cook for the little boy all day long. The old woman checked every day to see how much weight the little boy had gained.

"Show me your finger!" she would say, but the little boy was clever, and always showed her a thin little stick instead of his finger.

"The more you eat, the thinner you get!" said the witch angrily. After a month of waiting, she'd had enough.

"Light the fire!" she told the little girl. "Today we'll have a special feast!"

15

Would you like to know what kind of feast the witch had in mind? Go to page… **24**

Would you rather the witch left the children alone and played her nasty tricks on someone else? Go to page… **17**

he little boy wandered through the forest until he came to a magnificent castle, where he saw the sad face of a little girl in the window of the highest room in the tower. The little boy cast his fishing line. The hook stuck in the windowsill, and he climbed up. The little girl was very happy to see him, but a minute later she had to hide him in a cupboard when the horrible creature keeping her prisoner stomped into the room and ran to the open window.

He noticed the fishing line. "What is that? Who was here?" he howled. He started to climb down, but the line broke, and the horrible creature fell, breaking into a thousand little pieces.

Are you interested in what the little boy and the little girl did once the horrible creature was gone? Go to page… **10**

Or, would you be more interested in seeing what happened to the girl if nobody rescued her? Go to page… **25**

**16**

the witch, dressed like a little old lady, was walking toward the magnificent castle in the middle of the forest, with a basket full of apples. Soon she met a little boy carrying a fishing pole.

"A very good day to you, little boy!" she called. But the little boy just stuck his fishing hook into the nicest apple in her basket and reeled it in.

"Go on, eat it, lovey!" chuckled the old lady. The boy took a bite of the apple, and immediately turned into an ugly frog. Horrified, he jumped into the nearby lake.

## 17

Would you like to know what happened to the little boy who was turned into a frog? Go to page… **21**

Or, would you like the little boy with the fishing pole to catch fish instead of being rude to old ladies? Go to page… **5**

"**Y**ou're going to eat me?" stammered the little boy. "What kind of thank you is that?"

"It's a thank you for having to wait so long!" growled the horrible creature. "If you had saved me a thousand years ago I would have given you anything you wanted, but now…"

"You would have given me anything?" interrupted the little boy. "Are you really that powerful?"

"Of course!" snorted the horrible creature. "I can do anything!"

"I don't believe you!" said the little boy. "I bet you can't get back into the bottle!"

"Nothing easier!" laughed the horrible creature, and squeezed himself back into the bottle.

The little boy quickly put the top back on, then threw the bottle into the bushes and continued on.

Are you glad the story with the horrible creature ended like this? Then it's time to close the book, and turn to the back cover.

12

If you would like to know if anything else happened to the little boy in the forest, go to page…

18

One day, the three little pigs who lived in the forest each decided to build a house. The youngest pig, who liked to play instead of wasting time working, quickly built himself a house made out of straw.

The second pig didn't like to work much either. He picked up some sticks and twigs and used them to build a rickety, little house.

The third and oldest pig started slowly, and he carefully built a house out of the largest stones he could find. "You go on laughing!" he said to the younger pigs, who were dancing around, and making fun of him.

"There's a big, bad wolf wandering around this forest. We'll see who is laughing after he finds us!"

19

Whose house was best? The pigs' who didn't want to waste time working, or the oldest pig's? Go to page… 23

Would you be more interested in reading a different story? Would you like one about a witch who lived in the forest? See page… 17

even dwarves arrived home after a hard day spent working in the mine.

"Who's been moving our things and eating our porridge?"

They were grumbling and complaining when all of a sudden they stopped, speechless. There was a little girl in one of their beds! The dwarves stared at her silently until the little girl opened her eyes and explained to the surprised dwarves how she came to be in their house. She told them how she had run away from horrible creatures chasing her through the forest.

"Stay with us!" the dwarves cried. "Take care of us and our house, and we will always protect you!"

Do you want the little girl to accept the invitation and stay with the dwarves? Turn to page… **14**

Or, did the little girl say goodbye to the dwarves and find a new way home? Go to page… **21**

**20**

t he little girl, who had wandered deep into the forest, came to the side of a lake. She bent down to wash her face, and her gold bracelet slid off her wrist and fell into the water. The little girl started to cry.

An ugly frog popped its head out of the water and asked, "Will you give me a kiss if I bring you your bracelet?"

The little girl nodded, hoping she could somehow get her bracelet without having to give him a kiss.

The ugly frog dove down and soon came back with the bracelet. The little girl quickly put it on, and stared, horrified, at the frog offering its face for a kiss.

**21**

Would you like to know if the little girl kissed the ugly frog? Go to page… **9**

Or, would you like a story in which the little girl meets animals other than ugly frogs? Go to page… **4**

t he big, bad wolf moaned as he slowly made his way to the nearby lake, holding onto his sore stomach. He wasn't feeling well and decided to get something to drink. When he leaned over the water he lost his balance and fell in, disappearing forever to the bottom of the lake and no longer bothering the people and creatures of the forest. The grandmother and the little girl lived happily ever after, never thinking about the big, bad wolf.

Are you happy the big, bad wolf is gone? Then it's time to close the book and turn to the back cover.

You're not tired of stories, and you'd like to read more? Try another one on page... 2

he big, bad wolf, wandering hungrily through the forest, came across a meadow, where two pigs were dancing and singing.

Seeing the big, bad wolf, the pigs ran into their houses and locked the doors. But the big, bad wolf simply took a deep breath, and blew the two houses down. The pigs ran squealing into the older pig's stone house. The big, bad wolf could not blow down stones! He tried to climb down through the chimney, but he slipped and fell straight into a pot of soup that was boiling on the fire.

The big, bad wolf ran back into the forest, his bottom burnt, and never came back to bother the pigs again.

Would you like to know what naughty things the big, bad wolf with the burnt bottom did in the forest? See page… 4

Have you had enough stories with wolves? Do you prefer stories with witches? Go to page… 17

the witch, who liked to invite children into her house in order to eat them, happily hobbled over to the fireplace.

"We'll have a nice roast," she said, smacking her lips as she turned to the little boy in the cage. She pushed away the little girl, who was trembling in front of the fireplace, and bent over to poke at the fire. The little girl gathered all her courage and pushed the witch into the flames!

The witch never frightened children lost in the forest again.

Are you happy that the witch is gone? You must be ready to close the book, and turn to the back cover.

Would you like to know what happened to the little boy and the little girl who escaped from the witch? Go to page…

27

24

the horrible creature brought the little girl the most delicious foods and the nicest toys. He told her interesting stories and sang her beautiful songs, but the little girl just became sadder and sadder.

"You may go back to your home if you miss it so much," the horrible creature finally said in despair. "But you must promise me you'll come back in exactly one year!"

The little girl ran home happily, and didn't even think about going back to see the horrible creature.

Many years later, when she had nearly forgotten about him, she went to pick flowers in the forest. She was horrified to see the horrible creature lying among the flowers in a small meadow. "You never came back!" he said quietly. "And now I'm dying." He was tiny, and helpless. The little girl felt so sorry for him that she closed her eyes, and kissed him.

**25**

Would you like to know what happened when the little girl kissed the dying creature? Continue to page… **28**

What would have happened if the little girl had shut the creature in a bottle – just in case – and run away? Go to page… **13**

When the dwarves came home they found the girl lying by the front door, quite still, and they saw the witch hurrying off into the forest. They rushed angrily after the witch, but she ran to her house, and locked herself in. Distraught, they returned to the girl. There seemed to be nothing they could do to help her. Finally, they built a beautiful glass bed, and took the girl to a nearby meadow filled with flowers. The news of the sleeping beauty spread throughout the land and reached the ears of the young prince. Thoughts of the beautiful girl gave him no peace until finally, he saddled his horse and rode off to find her. After a long time, he came to the meadow. Overcome by the girl's beauty, he bent down and kissed her.

Would you like to know what happened after the prince kissed the sleeping beauty? Continue to page… **28**

Or, do you want to find out how the witch was punished for her wickedness? Go to page… **24**

the little boy and the little girl searched the witch's house and filled their pockets with the many gold coins they found hidden there. Then, they happily started for home. They walked and walked and just as they thought they'd never get there, they saw their village in the distance. The children ran to their parents, who cried with happiness. They had been sure something terrible had happened to the little boy and the little girl in the forest and that they would never see them again.

When the children took the gold coins from their pockets, everyone was stunned.

"Our whole village can live on these riches!" they shouted. And that is exactly what happened.

27

Are you glad that the children made it home safely? Have you had enough? Then close the book, and turn to the back cover.

Would you like another story? Turn back and start a new one on page…

17

The little girl opened her eyes and gasped. In front of her was a handsome prince, riding a white horse. They rode off together to his magnificent castle in the land of plenty, where they lived happily ever after.

Are you glad that the girl went with the prince? If you've had enough, it's time to close the book and turn to the back cover.

Are you still not tired of stories? Would you like to read another one? Start again on page… **19**

**28**

Lila Prap

Text and illustrations